The Fourth of July

Ira Wood

Rosen Classroom Books and Materials
New York

The Fourth of July is the birthday of the United States of America. The United States was formed on July 4, 1776.

Heroes, like George Washington, fought so America could be free from England. We **honor** these heroes on the Fourth of July.

We fly the American flag on the
Fourth of July. Our flag is red,
white, and blue. It has fifty stars
and thirteen stripes.

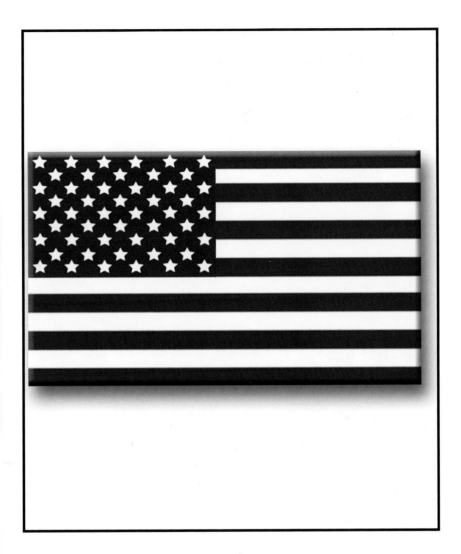

The stripes on the American flag stand for the first thirteen states. The stars stand for the fifty states in America today.

Many towns and cities have
parades on the Fourth of July.
Bands and dancers march in
Fourth of July parades.

Many Americans listen to songs like "America the Beautiful" on the Fourth of July. Bands play these songs in parades.

Many Americans play games
on the Fourth of July. We like to
play football.

Many people have **cookouts**
on the Fourth of July. We eat
fun foods, like hamburgers and
apple pie.

Many Americans watch **fireworks** together on the Fourth of July. Fireworks light up the night sky with lots of colors!

The Fourth of July is one of the most important holidays in the United States. We show that we are **proud** to live in America!

Glossary

cookout A meal made and eaten outdoors.

fireworks Tiny rockets that are shot high into the sky. They make loud noises and show us colorful lights.

hero Someone remembered for his or her great deeds.

honor To give special attention to someone or something.

parade A group of people marching down a street, usually to music.

proud To feel good about yourself or things that have something to do with you.